# Put Beginning Readers on the Right Track with
## ALL ABOARD READING™

The All Aboard Reading series is especially for beginning readers. Written by noted authors and illustrated in full color, these are books that children really and truly *want* to read—books to excite their imagination, tickle their funny bone, expand their interests, and support their feelings. With four different reading levels, All Aboard Reading lets you choose which books are most appropriate for your children and their growing abilities.

### Picture Readers—for Ages 3 to 6
Picture Readers have super-simple texts, with many nouns appearing as rebus pictures. At the end of each book are 24 flash cards—on one side is the rebus picture; on the other side is the written-out word.

### Level 1—for Preschool through First-Grade Children
Level 1 books have very few lines per page, very large type, easy words, lots of repetition, and pictures with visual "cues" to help children figure out the words on the page.

### Level 2—for First-Grade to Third-Grade Children
Level 2 books are printed in slightly smaller type than Level 1 books. The stories are more complex, but there is still lots of repetition in the text, and many pictures. The sentences are quite simple and are broken up into short lines to make reading easier.

### Level 3—for Second-Grade through Third-Grade Children
Level 3 books have considerably longer texts, harder words, and more complicated sentences.

All Aboard for happy reading!

For Natalie and Caitlin — J.O'C.

To the biggest copycat I know —
my sister Vicki — D.D-R.

*Library of Congress Cataloging-in-Publication Data*

O'Connor, Jane.
    Nina, Nina, and the copycat ballerina / by Jane O'Connor ; illustrated by DyAnne DiSalvo-Ryan.
        p. cm -- (All aboard reading. Level 1)
    Summary: When a young girl starts dance class with another girl who has the same name, she is upset that the other girl copies everything she does.
    [1. Ballet dancing--Fiction. 2. Imitation--Fiction.] I. DiSalvo Ryan, DyAnne, ill. II. Title. III. Series

PZ7.O222 Nf 2000
[E]--dc21                                                                                  99-48179

ISBN: 0-448-42152-6 (GB)      B C D E F G H I J
ISBN: 0-448-42151-8 (pb)      B C D E F G H I J

ALL
ABOARD
READING™

Level 1
Preschool-Grade 1

# Nina, Nina, and the COPYCAT BALLERINA

By Jane O'Connor
Illustrated by DyAnne DiSalvo-Ryan

Grosset & Dunlap • New York

This is Nina.

And this is Nina, too.

She is new at dance class.

Miss Dawn says,

"I will call you Nina 1 and Nina 2."

Nina 2 is a good dancer.

And she is nice.

She helps Nina 1 with her splits.

After class,
she always shares
her candy bar.

But there is
one bad thing
about Nina 2.
She is a copycat.
She gets the same
leotard as Nina 1,
the same
leg warmers,
and the same
dance bag
with a key chain.

"Look!" Nina 2 says one day.
She takes off her hat.
"My hair is like yours!"
says Nina 2.
"Now we can be like twins."
Nina 1 does not say anything.
She does not want
to be like twins.
She wants to be just herself—
Nina.

That day Miss Dawn
tells the class about
the next dance show.
"Each of you will make up
your very own dance."

Nina is excited.

In the car she tells her mom,
"We have to think up
all the steps.
The dance can be a solo.
That means you do it
by yourself.
Or it can be a duet—
that means you do it
with another kid."

At home Nina thinks
about her dance.
Yes! She has a cool idea.
She finds an old wand.

She tapes on ribbons.

She will do a solo.

She will be a rainbow!

At the next class,

Jody and Ann work on a duet.

They are puppets on strings.

Eric is doing a solo.

He is a karate guy.

He does kicks and twirls

and a back flip!

Nina works on her dance.

She runs and leaps.

Then she runs and leaps

some more.

"Very nice," says Miss Dawn.
"But try to put more steps
in your dance."

In the dressing room,
Nina 2 comes up to her.
"I'm not sure
what my dance will be.
Maybe I will be a rainbow, too."

All of a sudden Nina gets mad.

Very mad.

"No!" she says.

"That's <u>my</u> idea.

And you can't copy it."

Nina 2's face gets all red.

Nina 1 gets her dance bag
and walks away.

All week Nina tries to make
her dance better.
She does not think
about the other Nina.
She sees herself
in the mirror.
She tries twirls.
No good.

She tries splits. No good.

She ends up poking herself
in the tummy.

It does not hurt that much.

But Nina starts to cry.

"My dance is dumb,"
she says to her mom.
Then she cries harder.
She tells Mom about Nina 2.
"I feel bad. I was mean.
But she is such a copycat."
Mom understands.
"Tell her that you're sorry.
But also tell her how you feel."
Nina wants to.
But that is hard...
even harder than doing
a good split.

She waits for Nina 2
at dance class.
"I am sorry I yelled,"
she says. "I <u>like</u> you.
It's just—"

Nina 2 stops her.

"It's okay.  I am sorry, too.

I will stop being a big copycat."

They both laugh.

Nina 2 smiles.

"Too bad I can't do

a dance about a copycat."

Later in class
Nina 2 comes up to Nina 1.
She has an idea for a dance—
a duet.
Nina 1 thinks
the idea is great.

It will be cooler than her
dumb rainbow dance.
So they talk to Miss Dawn.

They spend the day together.
Nina 1 has good ideas
for the costumes.

Nina 2 has good ideas
for the dance steps.

They work hard together.
They have fun together, too.

At last it is the day of the show.

Nina 1 and Nina 2 do their duet.

Nina 1 is a black cat.

Nina 2 is the same black cat
in a mirror.

They pounce.

They prance.

They paw at each other.

At the end
everybody claps and claps.
Sometimes it is fun
to be a copycat!